Revenge

by

Eric Brown

BIRMINGHAM CITY COUNCIL (CBC)	
SPRING HILL	
HJ	21/09/2007
THR	£5.99

First published in 2007 in Great Britain by
Barrington Stoke Ltd
18 Walker St, Edinburgh, EH3 7LP

www.barringtonstoke.co.uk

ISBN: 978-1-84299-500-6 √

Printed in Great Britain by Bell & Bain Ltd

Barrington Stoke acknowledges subsidy from the Scottish
Arts Council towards the publication of this volume

Scottish
Arts Council

A Note from the Author

Stories are never easy to write, but some stories are harder than others. Revenge began ten years ago as a short story. I wanted to write about someone who made a silly mistake and lived to regret it.

In the story, the footballer imprisons a burglar in his basement – but what happens next? As the days pass, does the footballer let the burglar out? Does he keep him locked up? And what would happen to the footballer if the burglar escaped?

The idea was too big for a short story. A few years ago I re-wrote it to become a film – but I couldn't find an ending I was happy with. Then I came up with an ending that I liked, and I wrote *Revenge* in a week. All in all I've spent years, on and off, thinking about *Revenge*.

I hope you think it was worth it.

To Josh Lacey, with thanks.

Contents

1   Burglar   1

2   Fight   11

3   Victory   22

4   Nutter   31

5   Truce?   45

6   Tessa   57

7   Gun   68

8   Escape   82

9   Chase   89

10   Hospital   109

Chapter 1

Burglar

Dan Radford walked out of the City dressing rooms and crossed the car park. A crowd of reporters and photographers stood near his car.

"Hey, Dan. Is it true? You leaving City?" one of them said.

Another reporter said, "Have United made you an offer? Is it true, Dan? Are you walking out on City?"

Dan wanted to tell the bastards to sod off. Instead he ignored them. He walked round the reporters and dumped his bag in the back of his BMW.

A reporter stepped in front of him. The man looked like a rat. "I've heard you've had a fight with the manager, Dan? You don't like playing on the wing, right? You and the manager had a little tiff, yeah?"

Dan looked at the reporter. The others watched Dan, waiting for him to speak.

He felt anger boil inside him. "The manager and me get on fine, OK? I don't mind where I play for City."

"But you are thinking of leaving, yeah?"

It was a lie. He was happy at City. He'd never think of leaving City and going over to United. City and United were enemies. A City player never moved across to United. Dan had supported City all his life. When he had joined them last year, it had been like a dream come true.

He stared at the Rat. "It's bollocks, mate. I'm staying with City."

He got into the car and slammed the door. Seconds later he drove from the car park, swearing to himself.

It was a great life, being a pro footballer with one of the biggest clubs in the country. It was fantastic to be paid for what he liked doing best, and paid good money too.

There were only two things he didn't like about the beautiful game.

One thing was being injured, of course.

And the other thing was reporters. They were the scum of the earth. The things they'd do to get a story. And when they couldn't get a story, they'd make one up.

Last year, when he'd lived in his old house in the city, he'd had reporters almost camping on his doorstep. They used to follow him everywhere, down the pub, into restaurants and night clubs.

In the end, it had driven his girl-friend, Kathy, to leave him. She'd had enough. Her life wasn't private any more. The TV and press made her nervous, jumpy. The final straw came when she'd gone out with the rubbish late one night and found a journalist going through the bin.

She'd walked out on Dan a few days later.

* * *

Dan drove south, out of the city.

It was Friday, and he had a game tomorrow. City were at home in the FA Cup to a non-league team. The club rules were that players didn't drink on Fridays before a game. If you were seen even going into a pub, the club would fine you.

It worked, most of the time.

Dan didn't drink much. He wasn't like some of the older players at the club, who were real boozers. But at times, when the press were hounding him, or when he got to thinking about Kathy and how she'd left him ... then he just had to have a pint.

He knew a quiet pub in the next village to where he lived. The land-lord didn't know who he was, and the pub was always empty in the afternoon. He'd been going there a lot over the last few weeks. So far none of the locals had seen who he was, drinking on his own in the corner of the main bar.

He walked into the pub, ordered a pint of bitter and carried it over to his favourite seat near the window.

After the training session, he was tired and thirsty. The pint slipped down like honey. He bought another, then sat and stared out of the window at his BMW.

The car made him think about last year.

He'd bought it just after he joined City. Kathy had been excited. She liked driving fast cars. Kathy was slim and blonde and worked as a temp for a big company in the city. Dan had met her three years ago, when he'd played for a small club in the second division. They'd met in a pub, and got talking. One of the things Dan liked about her was that she had no idea he was a footballer.

He'd told her on their third date, and Kathy had laughed. "Well, that doesn't impress me, Danny Boy. I hate football."

But she liked fast cars, and when he bought the BMW he'd given her the keys and they'd driven out into the country.

She'd taken him to a quiet lane and stopped the car, and they'd made love all afternoon.

He was on his fourth pint now.

It hurt, thinking about Kathy.

She had said that she didn't like the newspapers snooping round, trying to dig up things about her past. She didn't like being pointed at in the street. She wasn't herself, she was "Dan Radford's Blonde Bit".

They'd argued for a week or so, and then she'd found the reporter going through the rubbish in the bin outside and she'd snapped. She'd said she couldn't take it any more. She'd packed her bags and walked out.

Christ, how Dan hated reporters. The scum of the earth.

He moved to the bar. He walked carefully round the table and chairs, not too steady on his feet. He bought another pint. His fifth, sixth?

The bar was filling up, but no-one looked at him. He was just another young lad, drowning his sorrows.

He looked at his watch. The digital display was blurred. He'd had too much to drink.

Was it seven, eight o'clock? Anyway, it was getting dark outside.

Kathy ... Jesus, the way she had unhooked her bra and walked into his arms ...

He put his hands to his cheeks. They were wet with tears.

He needed to get home, go to bed. He had a big game tomorrow.

He stood up, swaying. There was no way he could drive like this. The barman looked across at him. "Taxi, mate?"

Dan nodded. "Taxi, great."

Five minutes later he made it outside, somehow, and into the back of the taxi. He could remember giving his address to the driver, and not much else. The drive through the country lanes was a blur. Minutes later the taxi stopped. Dan pulled a tenner from his pocket and gave it to the driver.

He got out. The taxi drove away, leaving him alone in the lane.

He stood, swaying, and stared at his house. It was a big place, set back in a massive garden with a high iron fence all round it.

He found his keys and unlocked the gate. He felt dizzy, and his head was spinning. He shouldn't have drunk so much, he told himself. He had a game tomorrow.

If the press found out that he'd got himself pissed before a match ...

Fuck the press, he thought, and laughed.

He staggered up the drive towards the porch. He fumbled with the front door key. A few minutes later he got the door open.

It was good to be home, but he wished Kathy was still with him.

Alone in a big, empty house ...

He turned on the light in the hall. Then he saw the broken glass on the floor. At first, he didn't understand what it meant. Had he somehow smashed the window next to the door?

He heard a sound in the kitchen.

He wasn't alone in the big house. Someone had broken in. A reporter, he thought. A bastard reporter had broken into his house!

Angry, he made his way along the hall and pushed through the door into the kitchen. He found the light switch and turned it on.

The man – the reporter, or the burglar, or whoever he was – stopped and turned and stared at Dan.

For a second, the two men faced each other.

Then the man yelled and attacked Dan.

Chapter 2

Fight

What do you do when you get home drunk and find a burglar in your kitchen? What do you do when that burglar attacks you?

Dan didn't have time to think. He was drunk. His reactions were slow. The man was rushing towards him, yelling.

But the odd thing was, Dan wasn't frightened. He was angry.

He was angry that some stranger had broken into his house.

He didn't think about turning and running away. He acted on instinct, like when he was in front of the goal and the ball came to him. He didn't think, he acted.

He swung a fist and hit the burglar in the belly. The man doubled up, gasping for breath. Dan stepped to the side, meaning to knee the bastard in the head. But the burglar recovered, swung round and pushed Dan across the room. Dan staggered and fell. Looking up from the floor, Dan saw the burglar dive on him.

The first punch hit Dan just above the eye. The second punch caught him on his cheek. Dan reached up, held onto the man's shirt, and pushed him backwards. The burglar just laughed and grabbed at Dan's hair. He lifted Dan's head and smashed it down against the stone floor.

Dan cried out, pain filling his head. His vision blurred. He felt the man roll off him, and when he looked up he saw the burglar stagger to his feet and lurch for the door.

Dan pushed himself to his feet and ran after the burglar. He was angry. He wasn't going to let the bastard get away that easily.

Then he saw the base-ball bat on the work-top. It wasn't his bat – the burglar must have brought it with him.

So Dan reached out and grabbed the bat and swung it hard at the burglar's head, just as the man was reaching out for the door handle.

The wood made a loud thunking sound on the burglar's head, and the man just stopped dead still, swaying a little. Then he turned, blood streaming down the side of his face.

Dan knew for sure that the man wasn't a reporter. He had a big face, with a bald head and a gold ear-ring in his left ear. His thick neck was covered with tattoos.

And he looked angry, like a bull.

"You little fucker!" the man cried, and dived at Dan.

Dan didn't have time to lift the base-ball bat and hit the man again.

The burglar grabbed Dan's shirt and the two men staggered across the kitchen. Dan hit the door to the cellar. It opened behind him and he felt himself falling. The burglar was still holding onto Dan, and the bastard fell with him. They tumbled down the stairs, Dan groaning as he thumped down the stone steps.

They came to the bottom. Dan rolled onto his hands and knees and dragged himself away from the burglar. He couldn't see a thing because the light was turned off.

Panting, he stood up. He heard sounds in the darkness. The burglar was getting to his feet, breathing hard and swearing. They were in the cellar, where the last owner had kept all his wine. There were two or three rooms down here, where Dan stored all his junk.

Then Dan felt something in his hand. He was still holding the base-ball bat.

He thought about what to do next.

He tried to see the burglar in the darkness, but he couldn't see a thing. He could still hear the man, perhaps a couple of metres away.

The bastard was cursing under his breath.

"I don't know where the fuck you are, Radford, but when I get you, you're dead meat! Hear that, Radford?"

Dan kept quiet, his heart hammering. So the burglar knew who he was. Dan Radford, the footballer who had just moved into the posh house on the hill.

Then Dan heard something. A small sound in the darkness. Seconds later, he knew what the sound was.

A cigarette lighter.

The burglar held the lighter in his left hand, the flame lighting his ugly face.

Now that he could see where the burglar was, Dan acted. He swung the base-ball bat with all his strength and hit the bastard's head.

The man groaned and fell. The lighter dropped from his grip and went out.

Dan found the light switch on the wall. When he turned on the light, he saw that the burglar was out cold on the floor.

Dan almost laughed. He felt shaky and frightened. He reached down and grabbed the burglar under the arms and dragged him along the corridor to the biggest room in the cellar. He kicked open the door and dragged the man inside. Then he stepped back out, closed the door and turned the key in the lock.

He turned off the light and found his way back to the stairs. He climbed them slowly. He would ring the police, tell them what had happened, and they would come and arrest the bastard.

He came to the kitchen. He was shaking, and he felt sick. Shock, he told himself. It wasn't every day that you had a fight with a mad burglar and locked him in your cellar.

He needed a drink. He kept a bottle of whisky on top of the fridge, for when he wanted to celebrate. He didn't want to celebrate now, he just needed to calm his nerves with a strong drink.

He got the bottle and a glass and carried it into the lounge.

He sat on the sofa and poured himself a big glass of whisky. His hand was shaking and he spilled the alcohol over the cushion. He laughed. Kathy would have told him off about that.

He looked up, across the room to where he still had her picture on top of the TV. She was smiling at him. Christ, she was so beautiful. Why had she left him?

It was something about him. She'd told Dan that he never spoke to her, never told her what he was feeling. She said he never opened up to her.

She wanted someone she could talk to, and Dan Radford had never been much good at talking.

He swallowed all the whisky in the glass and poured himself a second one. He drank it, and felt it burn down his throat. That was better. He felt OK now. He'd stopped shaking.

Serves the bastard right, he thought. He'd leave the bastard in the cellar all night and ring the police in the morning.

He poured himself another drink, and drank.

Then another, and another.

He looked across the room at the photo of Kathy, and swore at her.

Then he had another drink ... and passed out.

* * *

When he woke up, he was in bed.

He couldn't remember going to bed. The last thing he remembered, he had been in the lounge, shouting at Kathy's picture like a daft school-boy. Somehow he had dragged himself upstairs and into the bedroom.

He sat up. He was still dressed. His head throbbed. Christ, he must have had six pints last night, and half a bottle of whisky.

His head felt as if there was someone inside his skull, hitting it with a hammer.

He had a game today, a three o'clock kick-off.

What time was it now? He looked at the bedside clock. It was ten.

He was OK, then. He had plenty of time to get rid of his hang-over, drive to the ground and get ready for the game.

But he felt like shit now. All he wanted to do was go to sleep. He lay back on the bed and pulled the duvet over him. He closed his eyes and felt himself drifting off ...

The next time he woke up, he remembered the dream.

He had dreamed that he'd come home last night and found someone in the kitchen. They'd had a fight, and they'd fallen down the stairs. Then Dan had hit the intruder with some kind of bat, and locked him in the cellar.

In the dream, the man had a bald head, and tattoos, and looked like he'd bite the balls off a rottweiler just for fun.

Odd, what you dreamed sometimes.

Dan sat up and looked at the clock. It was eleven. He'd have a shower and drive over to the ground. He touched his head. It still hurt, but he felt a bit better.

He showered, and dressed in his match-day suit. He'd better have something to eat before he went out. He hurried downstairs and grabbed a couple of bananas from the kitchen. He walked along the hall and opened the front door. He saw the broken glass on the floor. The window next to the door was shattered.

That was odd. Perhaps he'd broken the window last night, when he was drunk.

He walked to the garage and opened the door. For a second, he wondered where the BMW was. Then he remembered – he'd left it at the pub last night and taken a taxi home.

He'd take the Porsche instead. He climbed in, started the engine and drove to the ground.

Chapter 3

Victory

Dan left the Porsche in the players' car park and walked across to the dressing room entrance.

He saw the Rat, the reporter he'd spoken to yesterday.

The Rat hurried across to Dan. "Think you'll win today?" the Rat asked.

"What do you think?"

"The readers want to know what *you* think – the famous Dan Radford," the Rat said. "Think you'll get a hat-trick?"

Dan pushed past the Rat and moved towards the door.

The Rat said, "Nice shiner, mate."

Dan turned. "What?"

The Rat grinned and pointed to Dan's right eye. "I said, nice shiner. Black eye. A beauty." He looked Dan up and down. "You look rough, mate. Had a good night out? Been in a fight?"

Dan put his hand to his right eye. It was swollen, and sore. "Bumped into a door," he said.

"Yeah," the Rat replied. "And I'm Elvis."

Dan thought about his swollen eye. What *had* happened last night? He'd been so drunk, he couldn't remember a thing.

He ignored the Rat, opened the dressing room door and stepped inside.

* * *

By the time the game kicked off, Dan was feeling better.

The stadium was full. It was City's first FA Cup game this season. They were playing Barton from the Nationwide Conference league, and it should have been an easy game for City. All the experts before the game said City should walk it, win three – or four-nil.

But the experts didn't have to play the game. Barton might have been part-timers, but they had something to prove. They were out to show the Premiership team that they were no push-overs. They fought like maniacs for every ball and dived into every tackle.

City had most of the play, but it was one of those days – the ball wouldn't go in the back of the net.

It was nil-nil at half-time.

In the dressing room, the manager gave the team talk.

"We're playing like a bunch of wankers," the manager said. "We aren't even making chances. Against this level of opposition, we should be making chances and putting them away." He looked around at the players. "OK, so this half we're playing four up front, so there's more support for Dan. Let's stuff these no-hopers, OK?"

City played better in the second half. Dan came close to scoring twice. The first time his header was tipped over the bar by the keeper. A minute later his 20-yard volley hit the post.

The crowd roared. They could sense that City were getting closer. It was only a matter of time before they scored the winner.

With ten minutes to go, Dan got the ball on the right wing and cut inside the defender. He was 30 yards out, too far away to take a pot at goal. There were no City players up front, so he had to go it alone. He sprinted, keeping the ball close to his feet. He jinked around one defender, then another. He was in the penalty area now, with the centre-half coming towards him.

He could try to curve the ball around the defender and the goal-keeper – but instead he dribbled the ball around the centre-half.

Only the keeper to beat now.

He felt excitement swelling in his chest.

The crowd roared him on ...

He made a run towards the keeper ...

He slipped the ball through the keeper's legs and watched it roll over the line and hit the back of the net.

He raised an arm and ran to the corner flag. The feeling of joy – this was why he played the beautiful game!

Then he was mobbed by his team-mates.

He ran back to his own half, waving at the crowd.

Five minutes later, City won a penalty for a foul in the box. Jerry Thomas, the captain, took the penalty and stroked the ball home, sending the keeper the wrong way.

Two-nil. It was all over.

With just one minute to go, Dan went up for a cross from the right wing. He saw the ball coming towards him. He would head it into the corner of the goal.

The defender went up at the same time and tried to kick the ball clear.

That was the last thing Dan remembered. He felt a blinding pain as the defender's boot crashed into the side of his head.

* * *

When Dan awoke, he was in a hospital bed.

He felt as if an elephant had stood on his head.

He looked around. Someone was sitting next to the bed. He recognised the man – a City official.

Dan remembered scoring the goal, and then Jerry's penalty ...

"What happened?"

The club official said, "The centre-half walloped you in the head. You were out cold for an hour. You had a scan. You'll be fine. The doctors thought it best to keep you here over-night."

"The game ...?" Dan asked.

The official smiled. "We won three-nil. And guess who we drew in the next round of the cup?"

"Not United?"

The official nodded. "United," he said.

Dan laughed and thought about the next round against the enemy, two weeks from now.

He sat up. He'd been kept in here over-night, so it must be Sunday. "When can I get out of here?" he asked.

"Just as soon as the doctor says you're fit enough. He's coming round in half an hour."

One hour later Dan dressed and left the hospital. The official drove him home. Dan felt fine. He remembered scoring the goal – his 20th of the season.

The official dropped Dan outside his house and he opened the gates and walked up the drive.

Sunday, a rest day. When he'd been with Kathy, on Sundays they had driven into the country and gone for a walk, then found a quiet restaurant and had lunch. Now he spent Sundays alone, reading through the sports pages of the newspapers.

He opened the front door and walked into the hall. He saw the glass on the floor, and remembered his dream.

Suddenly, he felt sick.

He ran down the hall, into the kitchen.

Had he dreamed the fight with the burglar on Friday night?

He stood very still, his heart beating like a drum. He could hear something.

It was a man, shouting, and the shouts were coming from the cellar.

Chapter 4

Nutter

Dan sat at the kitchen table and held his head in his hands. He was shaking and he needed a drink.

He hadn't been dreaming. There really was a burglar in the cellar. And he'd been there nearly two days.

What should he do?

OK, he said to himself. *Think about this in a calm and logical way.*

He could go down into the cellar, unlock the door, apologise to the burglar and let him out.

And the burglar would most likely beat him to a bloody pulp, or maybe even kill him. The man was built like a brick shit-house. Dan wouldn't stand a chance.

He could phone the police, as he should have done on Friday night instead of getting drunk. But if he rang the police now, they would ask him why he hadn't rung them earlier.

He could always tell them the truth – that he was drunk and thought he'd dreamed about the burglar.

But would they believe him?

Not bloody likely! They'd most likely think he'd kept the burglar in the cellar for two days on purpose, to teach him a lesson. They might even accuse him of false imprisonment, or even kidnapping.

OK, he wouldn't call the police.

So what could he do? He was back where he started.

He could always ignore the burglar.

But could he really do that? Could he leave the man down there, without food or water, to slowly starve to death and rot?

Of course not.

So if he couldn't let the man out, or leave him there, or call the police ... what could he do?

There was only one thing to do, he thought. He would have to go down into the cellar and talk to the man.

Taking a deep breath, Dan stood up and moved to the cellar door. He opened it and walked down the stairs. The burglar had stopped shouting. At the bottom of the steps, Dan stopped and listened. He couldn't hear anything. He reached out, found the light switch, and turned it on.

The light blinded him. He blinked, then saw the dusty passage, the piles of card-board boxes. In front of him was the thick wooden door of the cellar room where the burglar was locked up.

It was an old door, with iron bars in a square opening near the top.

The burglar was gripping the bars with his fists and staring out at Dan.

The look of anger on the man's face made Dan step back.

The burglar cried out, "If you don't let me out of here, you bastard, I swear I'll get out and kill you!"

Dan took a deep breath and stared at the man. "And if I let you out?"

The burglar showed his teeth. "Then I'll still kill you, you little fucker!"

Calmly, Dan leaned back against the wall and looked at the man.

He smiled and said, "I can't win either way, can I? So why should I let you out?"

"Because," the man said very slowly, "you're a shit-scared little git. And you don't want the newspapers to know that you locked me in here, right? You're a big name soccer star and if this got out, City would drop you."

"If what got out?" Dan asked. "That I locked up some animal who broke into my house and attacked me?"

The man grinned. It was a horrible sight, all crooked teeth and spit. "Locked me up for two days, haven't you? That's not self-defence, that's kidnapping."

"Bollocks," Dan said.

But, he thought, maybe the police would be on the burglar's side. He'd heard stories about home-owners attacking burglars, and ending up getting prosecuted for GBH.

35

The burglar said, "I have friends, know what I mean? Friends in the under-world. If I didn't kill you myself, I could give the word to a contact of mine and they'd blow you away like the little shit you are."

Dan's heart was pounding hard. He tried to look calm. "So you make a habit of breaking into people's homes and stealing their stuff, do you? That must make you feel great, really big. And if people disturb you while you're robbing, you attack them, right? What a way to make a living!"

"Fuck you, Radford," the man spat. "You live in this fucking posh pile, earning thousands a week for running after a fucking ball. It's disgusting!"

Dan laughed. "It's entertainment. People pay to be entertained. I have a skill, and I earn my money."

"Twenty fucking thousand quid a week, according to the papers!" the burglar said.

"In fact, it's 25."

"You arrogant little shit!"

Dan shrugged. "Anyway, I'd rather play football to earn my living than rob houses. But that's probably all you can do, isn't it? Ever had a real job?"

The burglar hit the door with his shoulder and cried out, "Just you wait, you little fucker! I'll make you wish you'd never been born!"

Dan turned towards the steps.

The man said, "Where the fuck do you think you're going?"

"I don't like your company," Dan said.

"You can't leave me down here!"

Dan laughed. "Frightened of the dark, are you? OK, I'll leave the light on."

He went up the steps. Behind him, the burglar swore at him at the top of his voice.

In the kitchen, Dan shut the cellar door and leaned against it. He could still hear the man's cries, but softer now.

Christ, he thought, *the man's a nut-case. A psycho. If I let him out ...* He didn't like to think about that. The nutter would cut off Dan's head and piss down his wind-pipe.

He needed a drink.

He hurried from the kitchen to the lounge. He found a bottle of whisky and a glass.

He stopped. The last thing he needed, he told himself, was alcohol. That was why he was in this mess. If he hadn't been legless on Friday night, he would have called the police right away and everything would have been sorted out by now.

What he needed was a long walk, to clear his head and let him think about what he was going to do next.

He found his coat and unlocked the front door.

He saw the Rat as soon as he stepped out of the house.

The reporter was peering into the lounge window. Just below it was a window near to the ground – the cellar window.

If the burglar started yelling now ...

"What the hell do you want?" Dan said.

The Rat moved away from the window. He was a thin little bastard with a balding head and a small ginger moustache. He pointed to the gates. "You left the gates open. I took it as a friendly invitation to come in and have a look around."

Dan said, "This is private property. If you don't get out of here, I'll call the police."

The Rat just stood in front of Dan, staring at him. "That's not a very friendly thing to do, Dan. I just saw the gate open, and thought you might want a quiet little chat."

"With you?" Dan said. He glanced at the cellar window. If the burglar heard their voices and began to shout for help, the reporter would hear him.

Dan moved away from the house. The reporter followed him.

"I thought you might like to tell me what's going on," the Rat said.

Dan froze. He stared at the reporter. "What do you mean?"

The Rat shrugged. "You tell me, Dan."

"I don't know what you're talking about."

The Rat laughed. "No? Listen, I've been in this business for 20 years. You might say I have a nose for a story. That's why they call me the Ferret at the paper."

"The Ferret?" Dan said. "Not the Rat?"

"No, Dan – the Ferret. I can smell a story from a mile away. And something tells me I'm onto something here."

"What makes you think ...?" Dan began. He could feel that his voice was shaking.

The Rat held up his thin hand. "One," he said, sticking out his thumb. "You turn up at the ground on Saturday morning looking like you've been in a fight – black eye, a bruise on your cheek. You looked shaken up, not your usual smart, well-dressed self." The Rat looked at Dan. "You looked worried. Something was up with you, I'd say."

"Look – "

"And then I come up here, see the gate open, look through the window and see a nearly empty bottle of whisky."

Dan sneered. "Big story, 'Dan Radford on the piss'. So what?"

"And then," the reporter said, watching Dan very closely, "I hear you talking with someone in the cellar. Arguing." The Rat smiled to himself.

Dan looked away. He was sweating, but he didn't want the Rat to see that he was on to something.

The Rat went on, "Now that's strange, I say to myself. I could have sworn that young Dan lives all on his lonesome, after your blonde bit walked out on you."

"Fuck you!"

"Touchy, touchy, Dan. Very touchy. As I was saying ... you live in this big house all by yourself. So who, I ask myself, could you be talking to?"

"You're imagining things. It was probably the TV."

"You keep a TV in the cellar, do you. Dan?"

Dan stopped himself from diving at the Rat and hitting him. He controlled his breathing and put his hand into his pocket for his mobile.

"If you don't get out of here, now," he said, "I'll call the police."

The Rat grinned his sickly grin. He held up both hands and walked away, backwards, to the gates. "Point taken, Dan. I don't want to stay where I'm not welcome, do I? Enjoy the rest of the day, Dan. And don't worry, I'll be in touch."

The bastard slipped through the gates and walked along the road to his car.

Dan watched him go, his heart beating fast.

The Rat was onto him. He knew that someone was in the cellar. But how long would it be before the Rat started to investigate and found out that a local thug had gone missing, and put two and two together?

Dan locked the gates, then went for a long walk.

Chapter 5

Truce?

It was dark when he got back.

This time, he made sure he locked the gates behind him. He let himself into the house, moved into the kitchen and sat down.

There was no sound from the burglar in the cellar.

Dan had thought about things for a long time on his walk, but he still didn't know what to do. The longer he kept the burglar

locked in the cellar, the more difficult it
would be to call the police.

If the bastard had a heart attack and died,
that would be the end of Dan's problems.

He could always leave the burglar down
there, let him starve to death.

The man was a thug, a criminal who cared
nothing about other people's property. Dan
would be doing society a big favour if he let
the bastard rot. There would be one less evil
thug in the world. The burglar would never
break into other people's houses again,
wouldn't beat people up just for fun.

But ...

Could Dan do that? Could he let the
burglar die down there?

If he did that, then he would never be able
to forget what he'd done. He would always
know that he had been responsible for the
death of another human being. What if the
man had a wife and kids who loved him? If

the burglar just vanished, his family and loved ones would never know what had happened to him. They would suffer for a long, long time.

But how long could he keep the burglar in the cellar?

He heard a shout. He moved to the cellar door and opened it.

"You bastard!" the burglar cried. "You're dead meat, Radford! Hear that? You're a dead man walking!"

The burglar went on shouting at the top of his voice. Dan's house was well away from the village, but what if people heard all the noise? What if the Rat decided to take another closer look and climbed over the fence? He'd hear the shouts and call the police.

Then Dan had an idea. There was one way to shut the bastard up. He opened a cupboard and pulled out a bottle of brandy. The burglar would be hungry by now, so Dan looked in the fridge and took out a packet of six pork pies.

He made his way down into the cellar.

The burglar stopped shouting when he saw Dan through the barred door.

"Let me out of here, you little shit!" the man yelled.

Dan stopped in front of the door. "Do I look like a fool?" he asked.

The man stared at him. His face was red with anger.

"I brought you some booze." Dan held out the brandy.

The burglar reached through the bars and grabbed the brandy. Then he lunged forward, trying to hit Dan with the bottle.

Dan stepped back quickly. He held up the packet of pies. "So you don't want these?"

"What the fuck do you think? I haven't had a bite to eat for two days!"

"So stand back and I'll put them through."

The burglar thought about it, then moved away from the door. Quickly Dan stepped forward and posted the pies through the bars.

The burglar picked up the packet, ripped it open and stuffed a pie into his mouth, chewing messily. He unscrewed the lid from the brandy and took a long drink. Liquid dribbled down his chin, along with bits of pork.

Still chewing, he said, "I've been thinking about things."

Dan looked at him. "And?"

"We're stuffed, ain't we?" said the burglar. "I mean, both of us. I'm stuck in here like some fucking animal, and you're in a bad position, yeah?"

Dan said, "On the whole, I'd rather be on this side of the door."

"Very funny. But you know what I mean. If anyone comes round here, they'll hear me yelling, right? And if you don't let me out, then sooner or later they'll start looking for me. I mean, the missus will be missing me soon."

Dan looked at the burglar. So he had a wife. "You've been in here two days," he said. "Wouldn't she have noticed already?"

The man grinned round a mouthful of chewed up pork and pastry. "I often go on the piss for two or three days, don't I? But if I'm not back soon, the bitch'll start moaning. She'll go to the police, report me missing."

Dan thought about it. He said, "I don't think they're likely to look here."

The man smiled, and Dan didn't like the look of the smile. "No?" the burglar said.

"You see, the missus knows I go thieving now and then, don't she? And just the other day, I says to her, 'I bet Radford's got some nice stuff in that big house of his.' So ... the missus isn't thick. She'll tell the pigs that I might be up here. They'll search the place and find me."

Dan felt sick.

The burglar laughed. "And when they find me, you'll be stuffed, mate. You see, I'll just claim I came round for a friendly chat. I'll say we had a drink, and then argued, and you went off your rocker, attacked me and locked me down here in a drunken rage." He shrugged. "It'll be my word against yours, mate. It'll look bad in court, won't it? Imagine the head-lines: 'Soccer Star Accused of Kidnap'."

Dan reached out to turn off the light. He'd heard enough. How soon would it be before the police began searching for the bastard?

"But," the burglar said.

Dan turned and stared at him. "But what?"

The burglar grinned. "But ... I have an idea. Want to hear it?"

Dan looked at him. "Go, on."

"We come to some agreement. What do they call it, a truce? You let me out of here, and I give you my word I won't tear your head off."

Dan laughed at him. "And I'm supposed to trust you on that, am I?"

The burglar nodded, serious. "Yeah, you are. You see, I won't tear your head off, or have any of my mates do you over, because you'll pay me 25 thousand quid, right?"

Dan stared at him. "You must be joking."

The burglar shook his head. "Oh, no, Dan. I'm not joking. I'm serious. Deadly serious. See, the way I look at it is, you've got nothing to lose, right? Sooner or later the cops'll find me, and then you'll be landed right in the shit, yeah? But if you let me out, give me 25 thousand quid in cash, then I'll walk away as happy as Larry. Does that make sense, Dan?"

Dan thought about it. £25,000. A week's wages. He could afford it, easily. But would the burglar keep his side of the bargain? Once the bastard was out of the cellar and had the cash, then he could go ahead and beat Dan to a pulp.

Dan said, "There's a big mistake in your thinking."

"Oh, and what's that?"

"I don't trust you. So I give you the cash – what's to stop you killing me then, or getting someone else to do it for you?"

"Dan, Dan ... I'm truly hurt that you don't trust me. OK, so how about this: you give me the cash in three parts: ten grand when you let me out, ten grand a week later, and five grand a week after that. If you fail to deliver at any time, I'll make you suffer."

Dan shook his head. "Even then, what's to stop you getting your revenge when I've paid the last five grand?"

The burglar laughed. "Radford, you're so full of yourself, ain't you? Look, I'll be 25 grand richer and I won't give a shit for a little git like you. You're beneath me, a fucking insect. I wouldn't dirty my boots kicking your head in. Wouldn't waste the effort!"

Dan just stared at the man. "I don't like it. Once you've got the cash, you'd simply get one of your mates to do me over. I don't like the idea of that."

The burglar flung back his head and laughed. "I was trying to make it easy for you, chum! OK, have it your own way – wait till I'm reported missing and the police find me. Then you'll be in the shit. And another thing – " He stopped and stared at Dan.

"What?" Dan asked.

The burglar gripped the bars with both fists and pressed his fat face through the gap. "Later, when all this is over, I'll come for you and put bullets through your fucking knees. See how many goals you score after that, pretty boy!"

Dan reached out and turned off the light. He fumbled his way to the stairs and climbed them quickly.

In the cellar, the burglar was laughing like a madman.

This time, Dan decided he needed a drink.

He sat on the sofa in the lounge and poured himself a whisky, then another.

He went over and over what the burglar had told him.

Could he trust the bastard? If he gave the burglar the cash, could he trust him to keep his side of the bargain and not kill or injure him?

Of course not. The burglar would want his revenge, one day.

But if the police searched the house and found the bastard in the cellar ...

Dan looked across the room at the photo of Kathy.

One thing was for certain, if Kathy had still been with him, none of this would have happened.

He finished the whisky, then dragged himself upstairs and into the bedroom.

Chapter 6

Tessa

Dan woke up late in the morning. The first thing he thought was: the burglar.

He had a shower and got dressed, then went down to the kitchen. The burglar in the cellar was silent. Dan made himself a coffee and turned on the radio. Five minutes later the news came on.

After the head-lines, the newsreader said, "Local news now. Police are still searching for builder Greg Bolton, who vanished from his home in Little Hambly on Friday evening. Bolton, 42, was recently released from prison where he was serving a six-month term for GBH. He was reported missing by a business friend when he failed to turn up for a meeting. Police said they cannot rule out a gang-land kidnapping ..."

Dan turned off the radio.

How long would it be, now, before the burglar's wife suggested to the police that they should search Dan's house?

So the burglar had a name. Greg Bolton. Recently released from prison ... well, that was a laugh. He was imprisoned again – he should be getting used to it by now!

Then Dan stopped smiling.

It was no joke. Things were getting deadly serious.

He stood up and looked around the room. The only thing to do was what he had done when Kathy had left him, and last year when his dad had died.

Hit the bottle.

Except, there was no more whisky in the house, and he'd given the last bottle of brandy to the bastard in the cellar.

OK, so he'd go down to the village pub and get loaded there.

* * *

He walked down to the pub, ordered a whisky and sat in the window seat. He drank and stared into space and wondered what the hell he was going to do now.

Perhaps he should do as Greg Bolton had suggested – let the bastard go, then pay him £25,000. Dan could always hire a body-guard to make sure Greg Bolton got nowhere near him.

Yes, perhaps that would be the best thing to do – before the police found the burglar and arrested Dan for kidnapping or false imprisonment.

He got up and went to the bar for another whisky.

There was only one other person in the pub, a woman sitting on a high stool at the bar. She smiled at Dan when he ordered his drink.

She was in her late 20s, blonde and attractive. She was well-dressed and wore a lot of gold and jewellery. She was drinking rum and Coke and smoking a cigarette.

She said, "I've seen you before somewhere."

Dan said, "I live in the village."

"No, I mean ... I'm sure I've seen you on TV."

People often came up to him and said this. Some people thought he was an actor, or even a pop star. His face was familiar.

He smiled and said, "I play for City. You've probably seen my picture in the paper."

"So you're Dan Radford. You've just moved into the big house on the hill, haven't you?"

"A few months ago."

"Little Hambly's nice," the woman said. "People are friendly. That's what I find. We're a community. You live up there alone?"

He nodded. He noticed that her rum and Coke was almost empty. He pointed at the glass. "Care for another?"

"I don't mind if I do. That's very kind of you."

He ordered her drink and sat at the bar next to her.

They chatted for a while about the village, the country-side. The woman said her name was Tessa. Dan liked her. She was open and friendly and easy to talk to.

"I hope you don't mind me saying," she said, resting her hand on his sleeve, "but I'm not a football fan. Wouldn't know City from United."

He smiled. "Good. I don't like it when people want to talk to me just because I play football."

They chatted for another hour. Dan made his drink last. He didn't want to get drunk now. He found Tessa very attractive. She made him forget all his troubles. For an hour, he was happy.

He asked her if she always came to the pub for an afternoon drink.

She laughed and said, "Never. But today is a special occasion."

"Don't tell me," he said. "It's your birthday, right?"

She shook her head. "Wrong."

"Tell me."

She shook her head. "Maybe one day, when I know you better."

He said, "That would be nice. What are you doing tonight?"

She nipped her tongue between her teeth, smiling at him. He found her very attractive. "That depends," she said. "What are you doing?"

Dan said, "Nothing. I'm free."

"As it happens, so am I. Tell you what, why don't you come round to my place? I can cook you a meal."

He nodded. "I'd love to."

She looked at her watch. "Heavens, I must fly. I said I'd meet a friend at three. See you tonight, around seven. I live in the big white house, three along from the pub."

She picked up her handbag from the bar and slipped off the stool, then took his hand and squeezed. Dan watched her go, smiling to himself.

Then he remembered the bastard, Greg Bolton, in his cellar. A black cloud settled over him. He paid the barman and left the pub.

* * *

He made sure the gates were locked behind him. He didn't want the Rat getting in again. He let himself into his house, and then he heard the man shouting. He went into the kitchen and stood beside the cellar door.

"Hey, Radford, you bastard! You're back! We need to talk!"

Dan thought about it, then opened the door and walked down the steps.

He remembered what he'd decided earlier
– that maybe he should let the burglar go,
and pay him £25,000.

But Dan had changed his mind. It was odd,
but meeting Tessa had done something to
him. She was friendly and attractive and she
had filled him with confidence.

He didn't want to give the bastard £25,000.

He turned on the light. Greg Bolton was
gripping the bars, staring out at Dan.

"What do you want?" Dan said.

"Have you thought about it? Are you
going to let me out? Give me the 25 grand,
and I won't say a thing, OK?"

Dan shook his head. "No way. I don't
trust you, Bolton."

The man stared at him. "You know my
name?"

Dan said, "Greg Bolton. 42. Small-time
criminal – "

"Less of the small-time, you bastard!"

"It was on the local radio."

Bolton smiled. "They'll be looking for me soon, Radford. It's only a matter of time."

Dan leaned against the wall. He'd just had a thought, and it made him smile. "OK, so what if they do find you?" he asked.

Bolton said, "The police will do you, mate. Kidnapping. False imprisonment."

"I've been thinking about that," Dan said. "I'll just say you broke in a few hours ago, and I was about to ring the police. I think they'll believe me, a well-known soccer star, rather than some lying ex-con. What do you think, Bolton?"

"You bastard!" Bolton cried, reaching through the bars and trying to grab Dan. "I swear I'll kill you!"

Dan turned off the light and went back up the stairs.

In the kitchen, he sat down and thought about it.

If the police did search the house, he could say that Bolton had broken in earlier today. But the trouble was, these days the police had ways of working these things out. They would examine the blood on Bolton's face, and on the base-ball bat, and work out that Bolton's head injury was caused days ago.

They would know that Dan was lying.

So he was back to where he'd started.

He left the kitchen, went upstairs and had a shower. He changed into his favourite shirt and suit.

For the next few hours he would try to forget Bolton, and have a good time with Tessa.

Chapter 7

Gun

The house was big. Two cars stood in the drive, a Jag and a Range Rover.

Tessa opened the door and smiled at Dan. She was wearing a tight-fitting red dress and she looked beautiful.

"Good to see you. Come in. A drink?"

"I'd love a beer," Dan said.

She took him into the big kitchen. She poured him a Stella and opened a bottle of white wine for herself.

Dan looked around the room. He was trying to work out if Tessa lived here alone. She wasn't wearing a wedding ring, but that didn't mean anything these days.

She cooked steak and chips. They ate in a big dining room and chatted about their lives. She wanted to know what it was like being a pro footballer. He told her that it had its highs and lows.

"The highs?" she asked.

He smiled. "I get to do what I love, playing football. And I get paid for it."

She looked at him over the rim of her glass. "And you must have women falling over themselves to get at you."

He shrugged. "Maybe, but I don't like those kinds of women."

She smiled and said, "And the lows? What are they?"

"Reporters, and how they make up stories, always trying to dig the dirt."

She laughed. "Maybe they'll find out about us, dining together?"

"Maybe. But I wouldn't worry about it that much." He stopped, then said, "Unless you're married, of course."

She didn't answer him.

He said, "Are you?"

She looked away. "Yes," she said in a small voice. "But not happily."

She smiled at him, then reached across the table and gripped his hand. "Dan, let's go upstairs," she whispered.

His heart beating fast, he stood up and moved around the table. He held her and they kissed, and seconds later she took off her dress. He picked her up and carried her upstairs to the bedroom.

* * *

She lay beside him and stroked his chest.

He smiled at her. She really was the most beautiful woman he had met for a long time. He could see that she was older than he had first thought. She was not in her late 20s – more like her mid-30s. Ten years older than Dan.

"How come a young, handsome man like you doesn't have anyone?" Tessa asked.

"I did, until earlier this year."

"What happened?" Tessa asked.

"Oh ... she left. It wasn't working."

"She must have been mad!"

He smiled. "You and your husband, are you separated?"

She shook her head. "We're still together, but not for long if I can help it. I just want the bastard out of my life."

Dan said, "That bad?"

"You wouldn't believe it. He's a thug. He's been beating me up for ... oh, for the past five years. Two years ago I asked for a divorce."

"What happened?"

She shook her head sadly. "He put me in hospital. Broke my arm. He said he'd kill me if I tried to leave him."

Dan reached out and touched her hand. "Have you thought of going to the police?"

Tessa just laughed. "Listen, you don't realise what kind of monster he is!" She looked at him. "Dan, six months ago he was jailed for GBH. While he was inside, I packed up and got out – moved down to London."

"But he found you, right?"

She nodded. "I don't know how he found me, but he did. When he was released from prison, he dragged me back here, beat me up again. But this time he didn't put me in hospital. He just beat me up till I was black and blue."

Dan gripped her hand. He knew something then. He knew how much he felt for this woman. She deserved better than the monster she was married to.

Dan said, "So what will happen? You said you won't be together much longer?"

She sat up in bed, hugging her legs. She looked suddenly upset. She stared at her toes, then turned her head and looked at him. "Dan, I have something to tell you."

He laughed. "What?"

She looked so serious. What on earth did she want to tell him?

"Dan ... Look, I don't know how to say this." She looked away and whispered, "When I saw you in the bar, I knew who you were. I'd seen you on TV."

He shrugged. "So? That's OK."

"Listen," she said. "I know what happened."

He stared at her, his heart beating fast. "Happened? I don't understand."

"My husband," Tessa said, her voice shaking, "is Greg Bolton."

Dan lay back and stared up at the ceiling. "Christ." He shook his head. He felt dizzy. He thought about it. "So ... I still don't get it. How do you know what happened?"

"Because on Saturday morning, Greg rang me on his mobile. He told me what happened, the fight with you. He told me he was locked in your cellar. Only ..." she laughed "... only, his card ran out half way through the call."

"Jesus," Dan said. If Greg Bolton had phoned one of his criminal friends, instead of his wife ...

Tessa said, "He told me where he was, told me to get in touch with one of his mates. Then the call ended."

Dan's mouth was suddenly dry. "What did you do?"

Tessa laughed. "Well, I didn't do what he wanted, did I? I hate his mates, they're the scum of the earth. As far as I was concerned, he could rot in the cellar."

Dan looked at her. "Tessa, why did you start talking to me in the bar?"

She touched his hand. "The truth? Because I liked the look of you, and you looked ... worried. I knew how you felt, with that bastard locked in your cellar."

Dan shook his head. "I left it too long to call the police. After I locked him in the cellar, I got drunk. The day after, I thought I'd dreamed it." He told her all about it, from beginning to end. "So what the hell am I going to do about him?"

She looked at him with her big eyes. "I have a dream, Dan. I want to be free. I want a life where I don't live in constant fear. I want the man I love to be a good person, not a monster."

Dan squeezed her hand. His heart was beating, fast.

She went on, "I've thought of everything, Dan. I've thought of every way to get rid of the bastard." She turned and looked at him. "And then I realised that there was only one thing I could do. But ..."

"What?"

Tessa rolled out of bed and padded across the room. She pulled open a drawer. She put her hand under a pile of clothes and took something out, then carried it back to the bed.

She laid it on the pillow beside Dan.

It was a gun.

"He keeps three or four in the house," Tessa said. "They make him feel safe, he says."

"Jesus Christ," Dan said.

Tessa said, "I've dreamed of doing it, Dan. I've dreamed of taking the gun and shooting him dead."

Dan stared at her. "I know he's a bastard, but killing him wouldn't help you."

She looked at him. "I know, Dan. I know that! It's just a dream, that's all. More than anything I want to get away from him, and after he beats me up, I just dream about taking the gun and ..."

She was crying now. He held her, feeling useless.

She looked up at Dan, tears streaming down her face. "Dan, this is what kind of man he is. Listen to me. I ... I always wanted children. I wanted a child so much. The trouble was, Greg didn't. He said he hated kids. Well, last year it happened. I fell pregnant ..." She broke down again, wiping the tears from her cheeks with her finger-

77

tips. "So when he found out, when I told him, he ... Do you know what he did, Dan?"

He held her and kissed the top of her head.

She said, "The bastard ... he beat me up, and when I was lying on the floor, screaming, he kicked me in the stomach again and again until I began to bleed."

He held her and rocked her like a child.

"I lost my baby, Dan! He killed my baby!"

"Shh, it's OK. It's all over now."

She pulled away from him and dried her eyes on the sheet.

"I want to be free, Dan! I want to lead a normal life. I want to love someone who really loves me."

* * *

They lay side by side for a long time, holding hands but saying nothing.

The gun lay between them, cold and black.

After a few minutes, he said, "So, what are we going to do? I mean, about me and you?"

She stroked his cheek. "I want to keep on seeing you, Dan. More than anything, I want you in my life." She laughed. "It's silly, but I feel I've known you for a long time."

Dan held her. "We'll go on seeing each other. Maybe ..." He began to say something.

She looked at him. "What?"

"Maybe you could leave him. I'll sell my house. We'll move somewhere where he can't find us ..."

Tessa just shook her head. "He'd find me, beat me up."

"OK, so we'll go on seeing each other. When he's away, you can come up to the house."

She smiled and lay her head on his chest, "I'd like that, Dan."

He stared up at the ceiling, thinking about things. After a moment, he said, "There's just one problem."

She looked at him. "What?"

Dan forced himself to laugh. "The bastard is still in my cellar. What am I going to do about him?"

Tessa said, "I have an idea."

"Let's hear it."

She reached out and picked up the gun. She held it out to him. "Take it. Go back to your house and tell him that you're going to let him out of the cellar."

"But ..." Dan began.

"Listen to me. Tell him you're going to let him out, but tell him that you're armed now. Show him the gun. Tell him that if he tries to get you, you'll shoot him. That might make him think twice about attacking you."

He stared at her. "Do you think it'll work?"

Tessa kissed him. "What else can you do, Dan?"

He smiled. He was about to say, "Shoot the bastard," but he knew he couldn't shoot anyone, not even Greg Bolton.

Maybe if he showed Bolton the gun, warned him that he'd use it if Bolton came after him ... maybe it would work.

He climbed out of bed and got dressed. "Wish me luck, Tessa," he said. He slipped the gun into his pocket, kissed Tessa one last time, and left the house.

Chapter 8

Escape

Dan opened the gates and drove up to his house.

He parked the car in the garage, then hurried across to the house. He stopped in front of the steps and stared at the big white door. His heart hammered in his chest and his mouth was dry.

He knew what he had to do, but this was going to be very hard.

He had to show Bolton the gun, and tell him he'd use it in future if Bolton came after him. Then he would let Bolton out of the cellar, and hope he went home like a good boy.

He unlocked the front door and stepped inside.

He moved into the kitchen, then opened the door and crept down the stairs into the cellar.

At the bottom of the steps, Dan reached out and turned on the light.

He felt for the gun in his pocket. It was ice cold.

Feeling sick, he moved to the barred door. Bolton was silent.

Dan peered through the bars into the room, but he couldn't see the bastard.

"Bolton," he called out.

No reply.

He called out again, louder this time. There was still no sound from behind the door. He looked through the bars again. It was dark in the room, and he couldn't see a thing.

He hurried up the steps and into the kitchen. He pulled open the cupboard under the sink and rooted around in it until he found his torch.

He made his way back down to the cellar. He turned on the torch and shone it through the bars. He moved the beam of light round the dusty room.

"Oh, Christ," Dan whispered to himself. "I don't believe it."

Greg Bolton wasn't there.

Dan pressed his face to the bars and looked into every corner of the room, but there was no sign of Bolton.

He pointed the torch at the far wall. At the top of the wall was a small, barred window.

But now the bars were missing.

Bolton had pulled the bars out, climbed up the wall and escaped. He was out there somewhere. Soon, he would be coming for Dan, out for revenge.

His mind was blank. He couldn't think. What should he do now?

He went back up the steps and walked across the kitchen. Where the hell was Bolton? He could be anywhere now. He could be somewhere in the house, lying in wait for Dan.

Then again, he could be waiting for Dan outside in the garden ...

Dan thought about it, then knew what to do. He would get his car from the garage and drive into the city. He'd find a hotel, hide there for a while, then contact Tessa and try to work something out.

He left the house and moved across to the garage.

Seconds later, his mobile rang.

It was Tessa, and she was sobbing. "Dan! Oh, God, Dan! What happened? The bastard turned up here five minutes ago! He knows – "

Dan felt dizzy. "Knows what?"

"About us. A friend of his saw you and me together today. He saw Greg just now and told him. Greg said he'd kill you. He's driving up in the Jag. Dan, be careful!"

Dan heard something. It was a car, coming up the lane. "I think he's here," he told Tessa.

"I'll ring the police!" she said. The phone went dead.

Dan thought about what to do next.

He could go back to the house, hide somewhere and wait for Bolton to arrive. But he had a better idea.

He decided to leave the gates open. He would hide in the bushes and watch Bolton come through the gates. When Bolton entered the house, Dan would get away through the front gates.

The sound of Bolton's Jag grew louder as it raced up the lane. Dan ran across the drive and moved behind a bush, hiding himself from view.

Seconds later the Jag turned into the drive and drove up to the house. Greg Bolton jumped out of the car and ran towards the front door. He kicked it open and raced inside.

Dan looked at the open gates. The easy thing to do now would be to run out through the gates and hide somewhere until the police arrived. He looked back at the house. There was no sign of Greg Bolton. But if Bolton was looking out of the window when Dan stepped out from the bushes, he would see Dan ...

He had a better idea. He would keep himself hidden in the bushes and make his way around to the back of the house. Behind the house was thick woodland. He would head into the woods and escape that way.

Taking a deep breath, he set off.

Chapter 9

Chase

Dan thought about the madman in his house. Greg Bolton wanted to kill him – and now he had two reasons for wanting Dan dead. Not only had Dan locked Bolton up in the cellar, but Dan had slept with his wife.

He ran. He dodged through the bushes. To his right was the house, with a maniac inside it. Dan took deep breaths and told himself that this was a training run. He wasn't running for his life. He was in City's training ground, doing laps with the rest of the team. Any second now the coach would tell them to up the pace ...

Dan passed the end of the house and paused. He was breathing more easily now. He peered through the bushes at the windows of the house. He could see into the lounge. There was no sign of movement inside.

He set off again, jogging through the wet leaves. To his right was the lawn at the back of the house. In the distance was the edge of the woods. In a few minutes he would reach the woods and safety. He would hide and wait until the police arrived.

He came to the edge of the woods a minute later and stopped running. He hid himself behind a tree, his heart beating fast, and peered around the tree trunk at the house.

A part of him said he should just go on running into the woods until he was safe. But another part of him wanted to remain where he was, until the police arrived, and watch them arrest Greg Bolton. He wanted to see the bastard dragged away by the cops.

There was a big glass conservatory at the back of the house. As Dan stared out from behind the tree, he saw movement behind the glass.

His heart almost missed a beat.

A dark figure stepped into the conservatory and walked across it to the glass wall. The figure stopped and stared out.

Greg Bolton was holding something in his right hand.

A gun.

Dan felt dizzy. Fear made his stomach turn. He knew that Bolton wanted him dead, but the sight of the bastard with the gun made the fact very real.

As Dan watched, Bolton reached out and opened the door. He stepped out onto the lawn and stared into the woods. He seemed to be looking directly at Dan.

Dan pulled his head back behind the tree and pressed himself against the trunk, sweating. Had the bastard seen him? And what should he do now? Stay where he was, or set off running and risk Bolton catching sight of him?

He reached into his pocket and gripped the cold metal of the gun. He pulled it out, looking at the weapon. The conservatory was about 100 metres away. There was no way that Dan could hit Bolton at that distance.

He gripped the gun. He would use it if Bolton came any closer ...

He decided to stay where he was, keep very still and not move a muscle. He was sure that Bolton would go back inside and search the rest of the house.

His heart thumped in his chest. He would wait five minutes, and then set off into woods. Surely in five minutes the bastard would have gone back into the house?

One – two – three ... he counted the seconds under his breath, wondering what the hell the bastard was doing now. More than anything he wanted to peer around the tree again, just to make sure that Bolton was no longer on the lawn.

But what if he was still there, and saw Dan?

Eight – nine – ten ...

His breathing sounded loud in his ears, so loud that he thought Bolton would hear him. He wondered why Bolton had come from the conservatory out onto the lawn. Had the bastard seen movement in the bushes, as Dan had run past the house? Was Bolton just checking in case Dan was hiding in the woods?

Fifteen – sixteen – seventeen ...

The seconds passed with agonising slowness.

Perhaps he should start running again now?

He wanted to peer around the tree, to see where Bolton was.

Don't do it, he said to himself. It would be madness to risk showing yourself now ...

But a part of him just had to take a look, to calm his fears that Bolton had seen him.

Taking a deep breath, Dan moved very slowly and looked around the tree.

He froze.

Sweet Jesus Christ!

Greg Bolton was walking quickly across the lawn. As Dan ducked back, Bolton shouted in triumph, and a second later a shot rang out through the cold air.

The bullet hit the tree with a loud thump.

Dan began running. He didn't even think about firing the gun.

He just ran.

* * *

He sprinted through the trees.

He heard another shot ring out, then another. Loud cries sounded between the shots. At one point Bolton yelled, "I'll fucking kill you, you bastard!"

Dan had never known such fear. If he made one mistake now, he would be dead. He had already made one stupid mistake – one more would be his last. He had to focus, and think ahead. One slip, one trip on the uneven ground, and Bolton would catch up with him.

He thought about stopping and aiming the gun at Bolton. But the fact was that he had never fired a gun before – and Bolton had.

Dan wouldn't stand a chance in a shoot-out.

He was a pro footballer, and very fit. Bolton was an over-weight, middle-aged thug – but he was armed with a gun.

Think ahead, Dan said to himself. What must he do to keep alive?

Run as fast as he could, to get away from the bastard ...

Make sure he didn't stumble and fall ...

He ran, focusing on each step.

When he had put as much distance between himself and Bolton as possible, he would try to find a safe hiding place.

He ran on, dodging at speed around the trees. Surely now he would be 100 metres ahead of the bastard? Even so, he could still hear Bolton's angry cries, and random gunshots.

Dan had come on long walks through this wood-land. He knew it well. A mile ahead, deep in the woods, were the ruins of an old church. It was over-grown with trees and bushes. If he got away from Bolton, he could hide in the church until the danger had passed.

He changed course, veering to the right and sprinting. The trees were even thicker here. He had to slow down, to avoid crashing into the trunks.

As he ran around a tree, his foot caught on something and he tripped. He went sprawling and dropped the gun.

He got to his feet. The ground was covered in dead leaves, and there was no sign of the gun. He bent down and pushed his hands through the leaves, searching for the gun.

Christ, he thought, *what a damned fool.*

He was wasting time, looking for the gun. Bolton would catch up with him in seconds.

He began running again, breathing hard. Fear filled his chest like ice.

Suddenly, the wood-land ended and he found himself in a clearing. The church was a few hundred yards beyond the clearing, on a small hill.

Dan left the cover of the trees and raced across the clearing.

He was halfway across when Bolton cried out, "Stop where you are, Radford, or I'll put a bullet in your back!"

Dan stopped running. It was the only thing he could do.

He couldn't believe that Bolton had caught up with him. He raised his arms in the air, trembling with fear.

Bolton shouted, "Right. Now, turn around."

Shaking, Dan turned. He saw Bolton. The bastard was standing at the edge of the clearing, holding the gun out in front of him in both hands. Bolton was breathing hard, his face red and soaked with sweat.

He stepped forward, the gun aimed at Dan's chest.

Bolton was grinning, and it was horrible to see.

I'm dead, Dan thought. This is how it all ends. What a pointless way to die, shot by some brainless thug in the middle of the woods.

Bolton said, "You thought you could out-run me, eh? You thought I was fat, 40 and unfit? Well, Mr Professional Fucking Footballer, think again. I've got you just where I want you, and I'm going to make you suffer."

Dan shook his head. He tried to speak, but his mouth was too dry. He swallowed and said, "Killing me won't do you any good, Bolton."

"Shut it, you little fucker!" Bolton said. "Killing you will make my day. I want nothing more than to see you slowly bleed to death."

"And you'll spend the rest of your life in prison."

Bolton flung back his head and laughed. "Do you think I'm afraid of prison? I've spent half my life inside, Radford. And anyway, I don't intend to let the police get me. I'm going to fill you full of bullets and then get rid of the body. I've got mates who're pretty fucking shit hot at getting rid of bodies, yeah?"

In desperation, Dan said, "Tessa rang the police. They'll have this place surrounded by now."

Bolton laughed. "Is that right? Well, I don't hear anything at the moment, do you?" He smiled nastily. "I think I have time to make you suffer, before the pigs turn up."

Dan said the first thing that came into his head, playing for time. "And how do you propose to get the body away from here? Carry it on your back?" He tried to sound mocking.

Bolton showed a lot of teeth in a smile that looked evil. "Get real, Radford. Carry your bloody corpse out of the woods like a prize fool? No, I'll simply kill you and bury the body, and come back for it when all the fuss has died down."

"It won't work, Bolton. The police will be crawling all over the area. They won't rest till they find me."

Bolton laughed. "Trying to find where you're buried in this place," he said, "will be like finding a needle in a fucking haystack."

Fear took hold of Dan. He knew that soon he would be dead. What could save him now? He looked around the clearing into the woods.

There was no sign of life, no sound of the police.

Bolton moved the gun. It was no longer pointing at Dan's chest. Perhaps Bolton was having second thoughts about killing him? Perhaps Bolton didn't want to spend the rest of his life behind bars, after all.

Dan should have known better.

Bolton was angry. Nothing would stop him getting his revenge.

Bolton said, "This one is for fucking my wife, you bastard."

And he pulled the trigger.

* * *

The next thing Dan knew, he was lying on the ground, staring up at the sky.

The gunshot still rang in his ears.

Seconds later, pain exploded in his right leg.

He cried out and tried to sit up. He pushed himself up on his elbows and stared down at his leg. What he saw made him cry out loud again.

The knee of his jeans was ripped and bloody. There was a hole the size of an egg in his knee-cap. Blood was welling up in the hole and pouring out onto the ground. He could see bits of flesh and white gristle hanging over the edge of the wound.

He could see it, but even now he couldn't believe what it meant.

Bolton had done it. He'd shot him.

Dan looked up.

Bolton was kneeling down in front of him, smiling. "What a fucking pity, what a great sodding pity. Isn't that the famous right leg that's scored a dozen goals in the last ten games? Look at it now, Radford? Take a good look and then say you're very, very sorry for shagging my wife."

Dan took a deep breath. Pain pounded through him. He managed to say, "Fuck you, Bolton."

The bastard laughed. "What does it feel like to know that you'll never run again, Radford? What does it feel like to know that your footballing days are over, eh?"

Dan looked into the man's eyes, determined not to show his fear. "You're going to kill me, Bolton. So of course I'll never run again."

"You arrogant little prick!"

Dan forced a smile. "I might be going to die, Bolton. But at least I'll die knowing that you'll spend the rest of your life in prison."

"Like hell!"

Dan went on, "Life in prison. Plenty of time to think about me and Tessa. Plenty of time to realise that she hates you and wishes you dead."

"As if I'm bothered about what the bitch thinks about me!"

Dan shook his head slowly and said, "I'm going to die, Bolton. But first I'll tell you what you are. You're a useless shit. You've done nothing in your life for anyone but yourself. You've robbed and brawled and you beat your wife. You must be very proud of yourself, very proud that the last thing you did was end the life of someone far more successful than yourself."

Bolton raised the gun again and pointed it at Dan.

"Shut it, Radford."

"You're a useless waste of space, Bolton."

"I said shut it!" Bolton cried, and pulled the trigger.

* * *

105

Dan was amazed that he was still alive.

The odd thing was, the pain was no worse now. He looked down at his left leg. The knee-cap was missing. All he could see was thick, pulsing blood and bits of gristle like fat maggots.

Dan shook his head and managed to smile. "You'll have to do better than that to shut me up, Bolton. You'll have to make a proper job of it. Or I'll just go on talking, telling you what a useless thug you are."

"Shut the fuck up, Radford!"

Dan went on, "You said you've spent half your life inside? So you couldn't even make a success of being a criminal!"

Dan stopped talking.

He thought he was seeing things. He looked past Bolton, to the edge of the woods. He could see someone standing there.

He was dying, and in his last moments he was seeing things.

He could see Tessa. She was standing on the edge of the clearing, staring at him with pain in her eyes. She looked so beautiful.

And she was holding a gun.

It was all a dream. Tessa was an angel, coming for him.

Bolton was staring at Dan's face. He could see Dan's amazed expression as he gazed towards the wood-land.

Bolton turned to look at what Dan could see.

Dan stared. The golden figure of Tessa, the sunlight shining on her blonde hair, quickly lifted the gun and fired once, twice, a third time ...

And Greg Bolton jerked as the bullets hit him, and he fell to the ground beside Dan with a thud.

Bolton stared at Tessa. A strange look crossed his face: he did not believe that Tessa, his wife, had shot him.

Bolton died seconds later, weeping with anger.

Dan reached out towards the golden figure at the edge of the clearing. The last thing he saw before he passed out was Tessa as she came to him.

Chapter 10

Hospital

Dan sat in the wheel-chair and stared through the window. He could see trees in the grounds of the hospital, and people walking round in the garden.

He'd had his second operation the day before. The pain still throbbed in his left leg. He wondered if he would ever walk again, or if he would spend the rest of his life in a wheel-chair.

He would never play football again, that was for sure. He'd thought a long time about that. He would never run onto the pitch on match day. He would never again score a goal, or hear the crowd chant his name. All that was over.

The surgeon walked into the room, and he was smiling.

"Good news, Dan," the surgeon said. "I've been looking at the X-rays. It will take a few more operations, but I think everything will be fine."

"You mean, I'll walk again?"

The surgeon nodded. "You'll be on your feet in a few months – but I'm afraid you'll never run again."

Dan nodded. "At least I won't be stuck in a wheel-chair for the rest of my life."

They chatted for a while, and then the surgeon shook his hand. "I'll see you tomorrow, Dan."

Dan sat alone for an hour, thinking about what life would be like when he got out of hospital. Everything would be different. He would no longer be a famous footballer. It was painful to think about – but he would get over it.

He had Tessa, after all.

He thought back to the clearing in the woods, when Greg Bolton had stood over him with a gun. If Tessa hadn't turned up then …

Dan told himself that he was lucky to be alive.

* * *

That afternoon, Tessa came to visit him.

They kissed. "Great to see you, Dan."

Tessa had visited him every day since the shooting, one month ago. In that time he had come to know and love Tessa Bolton. She was a strong woman who had been married to a thug far too long.

111

The police had arrested her after the shooting, and then released her on bail. Her lawyer said that she would get off with a suspended sentence for the manslaughter of her husband. She had acted to stop a murder, after all.

And when Dan got out of hospital ...

They had decided to sell their houses. Both houses held too many grim memories. They would buy a small place together and start a new life.

"How were the press?" Dan asked.

For the past week, reporters and TV crews had camped outside the hospital, wanting his story. They had followed Tessa home, demanding to talk to her. In the end, she had booked into a hotel under a false name, just to get away from the reporters and TV crews.

A week ago, a reporter had tried to sneak onto the ward, dressed in a white coat. He had got as far as the door of Dan's room before a nurse had ordered him away.

Now Tessa laughed. "Not so bad today. Only three of them outside the hospital." She took his hand and squeezed. "Have you seen the newspapers?"

"I don't bother with the rubbish," Dan said.

"Just as well!" Tessa said. "The things they're writing about me! You should see some of the stories. They said I was seeing you for six months before I shot my husband!"

"What did I always say? Reporters are the scum of the earth. If they can't find a story, they'll make one up." He looked at her. "Are you OK? All this attention ... it isn't getting to you?"

She kissed him. "Dan, what matters is that I've got you. No reporter will spoil that."

He smiled, and thought of Kathy, and how the reporters had frightened her away.

"I have a surprise, Dan," Tessa said now.

He tried to guess what the surprise might be. "Go on."

"I've just talked to your doctor," Tessa said. "He said I can take you out this afternoon. I've booked a table at a quiet restaurant."

"Fantastic. It'll be great to get out of this place for a while." He took her hand. "It'll be great to be with you."

Tessa took his wheel-chair and pushed it out of the room and along the hall. Dan wondered if the TV and press would still be gathered outside the hospital, waiting for news about City's star striker.

He might never again play football, but, once he was out of hospital and living a new life, he would never be bothered by reporters again.

Tessa pushed him through the front entrance.

There was just one reporter waiting outside.

It was the Rat.

"How do you feel, Dan?" the Rat asked. "What's it like to know you'll never play for City again?"

Dan stared at the Rat. Then he smiled. "To tell the truth," Dan said, "I've never felt happier."

The Rat just stared, his mouth hanging open.

Tessa laughed and pushed Dan towards her car, and Dan realised that it was really true. Dan Radford, crippled ex-soccer star, had never been happier in all his life.

Want *more?*

Dead Brigade

---

by

James Lovegrove

A new kind of soldier ...

This is the British Army of the future. Soldiers brought back from the dead to fight as robots.

The zombie army can learn.

They can kill.

The only thing they can't do is die.

Even if they want to ...

Want *more?*

Heroes

---

by

Anne Perry

Murder on the battlefield.

It's the First World War. Men are dying every day.

Hundreds of them, sometimes thousands.

But one death is different. One death is murder. How important is one murder among all the other dead?

How far will Joseph go to find the killer?

Want *more?*

Kill Clock

by

Allan Guthrie

Pearce's ex-girlfriend is back.

She needs twenty grand before midnight. Or she's dead.

She doesn't have the money. Nor does Pearce.

And time's running out. *Fast.*